Odd bird...

Jack's father picked up the chick in his large farmer's hands.
He examined one of Oliver's strange two-toed feet and looked at the length of his legs and of his neck and at his odd freckled markings.
Then he gave him to Jack to hold.

"I've seen a few chicks of one sort or another in my time," said Farmer Daw, "but never one like this fellow."

"I haven't asked you, Jack," said Mrs. Daw, "because I knew your father would. But now I think you'd better tell us. What is it?"

Gently Jack stroked Oliver's back, dry and warm again now.
"It's an ostrich," he said.

DICK KING-SMITH

The Cuckoo Child

Illustrated by LESLIE W. BOWMAN

Hyperion Paperbacks for Children
New York

Text © 1993 by Dick King-Smith.
Illustrations © 1993 by Leslie Bowman.
First published in 1991 by The Penguin Group, Penguin Books Ltd.,
27 Wrights Lane, London W8 5TZ, England.
All rights reserved. No part of this book may be used
or reproduced in any manner whatsoever without
written permission from the publisher.
Printed in the United States of America.
For information address Hyperion Books for Children, 114 Fifth Avenue,
New York, New York 10011.

First Hyperion Paperback edition: September 1994
3   5   7   9   10   8   6   4

Library of Congress Cataloging-in-Publication Data
King-Smith, Dick. The cuckoo child/Dick King-Smith;
illustrated by Leslie Bowman — 1st ed. p.   cm.
Summary: With the unknowing help of his pet geese,
eight-year-old Jack Daw decides to raise
an ostrich on his father's farm.
ISBN 1-56282-350-7 (trade)–ISBN 1-56282-351-5 (lib. bdg.)
ISBN 0-7868-1001-7 (pbk.)
[1. Ostriches–Fiction. 2. Geese–Fiction. 3. Farm life–Fiction.]
I. Bowman, Leslie W., ill. II. Title.
PZ7.K5893Ct 1993 [Fic] — dc20   92-72029   CIP AC

Contents

 # 1 Scrambled Eggs

"Are you warm enough?" said Jack's mother as she tucked him into bed. Jack nodded. After his mother had kissed him good night and gone out of the room, leaving the door ajar, he waited, listening.

He heard her footsteps going down the stairs and along the hallway to the kitchen, and then he sat up.

Twisting around, he lifted his pillows. Beneath them were three brown eggs.

"Are you warm enough?" said Jack.

Of all the animals on his father's farm, Jack liked the birds best. Farmer Daw's pride and joy was his herd of dairy cows; Mrs. Daw was particularly fond of the pigs; and Jack's big sister, Margery, was crazy about horses. But Jack's favorite creatures were birds.

Even as a helpless baby in his stroller he had gurgled with pleasure at the sight of the swallows darting across the summer sky or at the sound of a sparrow's *cheep* or a starling's whistle. And once he was old enough to stagger about the farm, he always headed straight for the poultry—the hens, the ducks, the geese, and the turkeys. Anything with feathers fascinated little Jack Daw.

Now, at four years of age, Jack was beginning to understand how birds are born. Eggs, he now knew, weren't just for people to eat. If you left them with the mother bird and she kept them warm, baby chicks would hatch out of them. Jack wasn't too sure how this happened or how long it would take.

"But I'll keep you warm, all right," he said to the three eggs. "Don't you worry about that."

Gently he put the pillows back on top of them. Carefully he laid his head on top of the pillows. Happily he went to sleep.

At first Jack slept peacefully, but sometime later in the night he had a strange dream. In it he found an egg, not an ordinary-size egg but a huge thing eight inches long, and out of it there hatched the strangest-looking baby bird that began to grow with nightmarish speed.

Before you could say "Jack Daw," let alone "Jack Robinson," the dream-chick's size increased until it stood half as tall again as a man and stared down at Jack with huge brown eyes.

Jack tossed and turned in his sleep as the nightmare gripped him, twisting his head from side to side on the pillows until at last he awoke. He looked wildly around and then, seeing to his great relief the familiar outlines of his own safe room, fell fast asleep again.

"Jack!" his mother called the next morning. "Are you awake? Breakfast is nearly ready."

Jack lay still for a moment, remembering his dream and then—and only then—remembering what lay beneath his pillows.

He lifted them and saw, on the sheet beneath, a horrid, sticky mess of shattered shell and slimy white and gooey golden yolk.

He heard his mother's voice again.

"Hurry up!" she called. "Or it'll get cold. It's scrambled eggs."

2) Lydia and Wilfred

At the time, Jack's mother was very angry—first with Jack, then with her husband for laughing, then with Margery for teasing Jack, and then with Jack for kicking Margery. Finally, after Farmer Daw had gone out to see to his cows, and Margery had gone off to school, and Jack had stomped off to tell the hens and ducks and geese and turkeys how unfair life was, Mrs. Daw was angry with herself for having made such a fuss.

All the same, while her son was brushing his teeth that evening, she couldn't resist having a peek under his pillows. But there was nothing there. Jack had a clean sheet.

"That boy and his birds!" Mrs. Daw said to her husband later. "Most children his age want animals like rabbits or guinea pigs. Jack spends all his time in the henhouse or by the duck pond or out in the orchard with the geese and the turkeys."

"If it's got feathers, Jack likes it," said Farmer Daw. "But he's got a lot to learn. Imagine trying to hatch eggs under his pillow overnight when it takes a hen three weeks! It's about time he had a lesson in chick rearing."

So the next morning, with Jack watching his every move like a hawk, Jack's father set a broody hen on a clutch of a dozen eggs.

Then, every day for the next twenty-one days, father and son went together to the broody-coop to take the hen off the eggs for ten minutes so that she could stretch her legs and make herself comfortable and eat some corn and drink some water. Jack was too small to lift the fluffed-out grumbling broody off the nest by himself, but he wasn't a bit scared of her, the farmer noticed, nor of the cockerel or any of the other poultry.

"Be careful she doesn't peck you," Farmer Daw said as Jack stroked the hen's ruffled feathers, but she never did.

When they came to the coop on the morning of the twenty-first day, Jack's father said, "Listen."

Jack listened and heard not just the clucking of the hen but a lot of little chirping sounds. He peered in through the bars and could see some little faces already peeking out from beneath the broody's skirts.

As luck would have it, it was a perfect hatch, for when the hen was taken out of the coop that afternoon, there in a mess of broken shells were a dozen tiny fluffy chicks.

"Count them, Jack," said Farmer Daw.

"One, two, three," said Jack, "five, seven, eight, nine, ten, twelve, thirteen, fifteen, sixteen."

His father laughed, stroking the hen in his arms. "Didn't she do well?" he said. "You know, I don't think you could have hatched your eggs even if you'd stayed in bed for three weeks and kept very still."

Very carefully Jack picked up one of the baby

chicks. He held it in front of his face and stared at it, fascinated.

"Daddy," he said, "when can I have some birds of my very own?"

"When you're five," said his father.

Jack's fifth birthday present was a pair of colorful budgerigars.

For his sixth he was given bantams.

For his seventh, ducks.

All of these thrived and multiplied.

Just as some people are specially skilled with plants—they are said to have "green thumbs," meaning that everything in their gardens does well—so Jack was good with birds. He had a way with them.

He looked after his budgies and his bantams and his ducks with great care, and they in turn seemed anxious to do their very best for him. Other people's birds might sit on eggs that turned out to be infertile and addled, or their chicks might be stillborn. But Jack's mother birds, of any sort, hardly ever lost a baby.

One morning the Daw family was sitting at the breakfast table, eating soft-boiled eggs (except for Jack, who for some years now had not been able to bring himself to do such a thing).

14

"You'll be eight soon," said his mother.

"Yes," said Jack.

"How about something different for a birthday present this time?" said his father.

"No," said Jack.

"You and your birds!" said Margery. "The older you get, the bigger *they* get. Budgies, bantams, ducks. I suppose it'll be geese next."

"Yes," said Jack. "A pair. Please."

"But we've got four geese out in the orchard as it is," said his father.

"That's just it," said Jack. "We've got four ancient old gray geese to graze the grass under the apple trees. But we haven't got a gander."

"So what?" said Margery.

Jack sighed.

"To have babies you need a daddy as well as a mommy," he said patiently. "Didn't you know?"

So on New Year's Day, which was Jack's birthday, a handsome young white gander and a beautiful young white goose arrived at the farm.

The gander was very protective of his mate and stretched his neck and flapped his wings and hissed angrily if anyone came near her or, indeed, near the four old gray geese in the orchard. Anyone, that is, except Jack. Unafraid as usual, he won their confidence immediately, and Wilfred and

15

Lydia, as he named them, were soon feeding from his hand and following everywhere at his heels with cries of pleasure.

A couple of months later, Lydia began to make a nest in the corner of an old shed that stood under one of the apple trees. She made it of grass and hay and straw and lined it with soft down plucked from her breast.

And then one day Jack came rushing in, grinning from ear to ear.

"Lydia's laid her first egg!" he said.

"A golden one, I suppose?" said Margery.

Jack sighed.

"That was just a fairy tale," he said patiently. "Didn't you know?"

"I bet that's the biggest egg you've ever seen in your life," said his father.

"Or ever will, I imagine," said his mother.

But there she was wrong.

The very next day, just at the moment when Lydia was laying the second of her clutch, Jack was staring openmouthed at a couple of dozen of the biggest eggs in the world!

3 Then There Were Eight

For weeks the boys and girls in Jack's class had been excited about a field trip to Wildlife Park. Most of the children were fond of animals anyway, and every one of them was looking forward to the bus ride and to eating their packed lunches and to spending their pocket money on all kinds of attractive and useless things in the souvenir shop.

Jack felt slightly differently.

Not that he didn't want to see the white rhinos and the giraffes and the zebras and the monkeys and all the other four-legged creatures. He just wished that the class could have gone instead to Birdland or Tropical Bird Gardens. Wildlife Park, he suspected, would not have many of his feathered friends.

However, when they arrived and began to walk around, he realized that there were more birds

18

than he had thought; there were peacocks that roamed the grounds, macaws that flew freely among the trees, and a flock of flamingos in a lake.

The children walked along, endlessly nagging their teacher to allow them to open their packed lunches ("I'm starving, Miss Bunting, it's been more than two hours since I had my breakfast") until they came to a point in a little wooded area where the path forked. Everyone took the right-hand way except Jack, who was dawdling at the back, daydreaming about Lydia and the chances of her laying a second egg today. Now, attracted by the sight of a peacock displaying, he took the left fork.

For a moment he stood with his back to a tall wire fence, watching the peacock, and then suddenly something told him that he himself was being watched. Slowly he turned, and there on the other side of the fence stood an extraordinary black-and-white bird, half as tall again as a man, staring down at him with huge brown eyes.

For a long moment they gazed at one another, the small boy and the great male ostrich. Then the spell was broken as Jack heard his name angrily called and saw his teacher beckoning to him from the fork in the path.

"How many times do you have to be told, Jack?" she said when he reached her. "Keep together, do you hear me?"

"Yes, Miss Bunting," said Jack. "But please, Miss Bunting, we've missed the ostriches."

The teacher looked at her map of Wildlife Park.

"No we haven't," she said. "We'll come to them later, after the rhinos."

Jack paid little attention to the rhinos, nor did he think of Lydia any longer. His mind was full of that magnificent giant bird, of its black feathering with white wing and tail plumes, of its massive legs and huge two-toed feet, of its long, long neck, and of those large brown heavily lashed eyes that had stared into his own with a look of such intelligence and understanding. He couldn't wait to see it again!

At last they came, by the correct route, to a sign that said

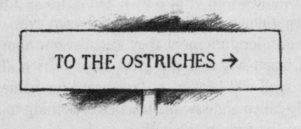

TO THE OSTRICHES →

and beside it was a printed notice.

The teacher made the children stop, and she read it to them.

OSTRICH (*Struthio camelus*)

The world's largest bird. The ostrich cannot fly but can run at speeds of up to 40 mph. Male ostriches can reach a height of 9 feet and weigh as much as 345 pounds. Females are smaller. The male is black and white, the female brownish. This color difference is an advantage when brooding eggs, for the hen sits on them by day, the cock by night. An ostrich egg can be 8 inches in length and 6 inches in diameter, and its shell can support the weight of a 280-pound man.

As the teacher finished reading, there was a jumble of voices.

"Nine feet high! That's half as tall again as my dad!"

"Three hundred and forty-five pounds! That's about three times as heavy as my mom."

"My uncle George weighs about 280 pounds—imagine him balancing on an egg!"

Amid all the noise, Jack pulled at the teacher's sleeve. "Miss Bunting, Miss Bunting!" he cried. "Do you think we'll see an ostrich egg?"

A man's voice answered, "You'll see lots of them.

In fact, if you hang on a few minutes, I'll bring some to show you."

Everybody looked around, and there was one of the park's rangers. He was pushing a small wheelbarrow containing some cabbages and some apples, and he walked off, saying, "Come along, children, follow me."

As soon as they reached the ostrich paddock they could see the eggs. There were a couple of dozen of them lying on the ground in a rough scooped-out hollow made in a patch of bare earth. Even the facts given on the notice had not really prepared the children for the size of the great yellowish white things.

"There!" said the ranger. "How'd you like one of them for your breakfast, eh? There's as much in one of them as in twenty-four hen eggs!"

The children gaped.

Jack raised his hand. "Please," he said, "why isn't one of the ostriches sitting on them?"

"Now, that's a good question, young man," said the ranger (and Jack's teacher looked pleased), "and I'll tell you the answer. We've got four ostriches here, three hens and a cock, and all the hens are laying right now, all in this same spot. And any day now I'm expecting one of them to go broody, and then she'll gather about fifteen of these eggs together and start sitting on them. Like it says on the notice, she'll sit by day and the cock will take over at night."

"But what about the other eggs?" asked Jack's teacher. "There are more than fifteen there."

"That's another good question, miss," said the ranger (and Jack's teacher looked even more pleased), "and I'll tell you the answer. I pick 'em up. The three hens lay such a lot at this time of year that if I didn't take some away, the broody bird might try to sit on too many—more than she or her mate could cover properly—and then none of them would be properly incubated. So every now and then I pick up the surplus ones."

While the man had been talking, the four ostriches had come striding up from a distant part of the paddock, and now the towering nine-foot male and his slightly smaller brown females stood by the wire, staring down at the children.

"But don't the birds object," said the teacher, "if you take some of the eggs?"

"They might, miss," said the ranger, "and a kick from an ostrich can kill a man, so I don't take any chances. If you and the children just stay here and watch, you'll see."

So they stayed and watched as the ranger walked off, pushing his wheelbarrow, while the four ostriches paced along inside the fence, their huge eyes fixed on the cabbages and apples.

When he had gone some way away, the ranger began to throw the fruit and vegetables over the fence. Then, leaving the birds busily feeding, he hurried back, unlocked the gate, and, pushing in the wheelbarrow, reloaded it with the more out-lying of the ostrich eggs.

Jack watched all this with mounting excitement. It might take a bird to hatch eggs, but a boy could hatch a *plan*! He unzipped the canvas backpack slung over his shoulder.

The ranger came out again and relocked the gate.

In the wheelbarrow were nine eggs.

He picked one up.

"Now," he said, "where's the young man who asked that question?" And when Jack raised his hand, the ranger said, "Here, you can go first," and handed him an ostrich egg.

Then, one after another, the ranger took the other spare eggs out of the wheelbarrow and gave them to various children to hold and examine.

"Let me!" "Let me!" "Give it here!" "Let me go first!" cried the boys and girls as they competed to hold an egg, and in the hubbub and confusion nobody noticed what Jack was doing or heard him zip his backpack shut.

"Now, now, children, that's enough!" said the teacher. "Put all the eggs back in the wheelbarrow now." She turned to the ranger and said, "What will you do with these?"

"Often we send some to other safari parks or zoos," said the ranger, "but actually these will be fed to our big snakes, the pythons and the boa constrictors. Now then, have you all put your eggs back?"

"Yes!" chorused the children.

Jack said nothing.

"Thank you for your trouble," said the teacher.

"Bye-bye then," said the ranger, and off he went.

In the wheelbarrow were eight eggs.

 **The Swap**

Outside the souvenir shop at Wildlife Park there were a number of wooden tables and benches, and here at last Jack's teacher, worn down by the pleas of her class, allowed the children to eat.

She divided them up, so many to each table, and then out from backpacks and knapsacks and satchels came the lunch boxes.

Instantly, like a large brood of nestling chicks, every mouth gaped open, and into each went sandwiches and cookies and apples and chocolate bars.

Jack had managed to position himself at one end, and he took his lunch box out of his backpack carefully, shielding the action with his body and then placing the backpack beside him on the bench. He began to eat a sandwich hungrily, yet hardly tasting it, so stunned was he by the excitement of what he had done.

Suddenly he heard his name called.

"Jack!" cried his teacher. "Move over a bit. Make room for Gary."

Before Jack could do anything, Gary, the largest, the greediest, and the stupidest boy in the class, plopped himself down right on top of Jack's backpack.

"Yow!" cried Gary, hoisting himself upright again and rubbing his fat bottom in mock agony. "What on earth do you have in there, Jack?"

Hastily Jack grabbed his backpack and put it on the ground, between his feet.

"It's a football," he said. "If you haven't burst it, you great big lump of lard! Why don't you watch what you're doing?" Gary's mouth was already too full to answer.

Jack used his feet to examine his hidden treasure as best he could. It still felt egg-shaped.

It still felt egg-shaped when they boarded the bus to return to school, and by then it had survived yet another assault.

After the class had finished lunch, the teacher allowed the children to run around in a play area before completing the tour of the park.

"Wish we had a football!" shouted one of the boys.

Gary, still eating, called out "Jack's got one!" and threw Jack's backpack on the grass.

"No!" cried Jack, but before he could rescue the backpack, someone took an almighty kick at it and then fell to the ground, clutching his foot.

"It'sh a hard one, innit!" said Gary with his mouth full. He sounded quite proud.

But it was nothing compared with Jack's pride when, safely back in his bedroom at the farm at the end of the day, he opened the backpack and took out the ostrich egg.

Breathlessly he examined every inch of its smooth yellowish surface, but there was no sign of a crack or blemish of any kind upon that shell that could support the weight of a 280-pound man.

The outside of the giant egg was perfect. And just think what Jack would find inside when that shell was finally broken!

All he had to do was to wait until Lydia had laid her full clutch of eggs and was starting to sit, and then he would slip his beautiful monster under her.

At that precise moment, as Jack was imagining the warmth beneath a broody goose, a thought struck him that made his blood run cold. What if the incubation period for ostrich eggs was different from that for goose eggs?

The hatching time varied according to the kind of bird, as he well knew from his own experience. Seventeen to eighteen days for a budgerigar egg,

twenty-one for a bantam's or any chicken's egg, twenty-eight days for a duck egg, and thirty days for a goose egg. But how long for an ostrich egg?

Quickly Jack pulled down his well-thumbed copy of *Birds of the World* from the bookshelf and scanned the index.

". . . Orange bird . . . Oriole . . . Ortolan . . . Osprey . . . Ostrich."

He turned to the right page.

There were all the facts, just as the notice in the park had said, but how long? Ah, there it was!

". . . Incubation period—five to six weeks."

Five to six weeks! From thirty-five to forty-two days! At thirty days Lydia's goslings would hatch, and Lydia would lead them out of the shed, and she and Wilfred would proudly parade around the orchard, showing off their children.

But in the deserted nest, growing colder by the moment, would lie the ostrich egg, perhaps a week or more short of hatching and, inside it, almost fully formed, an ostrich chick destined to die.

"No! No!" cried Jack out loud, cuddling his prize and stroking it as though the tiny germ of life inside it had already begun to develop. (It never occurred to him that the egg might possibly be infertile.)

"No, you *will* hatch, I promise you! I can always breed from Lydia and Wilfred another time, but

31

this is my only chance ever to have an ostrich of my very own."

He sat, thinking of the great cock that had stared down at him that morning and imagining his own ostrich looking just like that in a year or two's time. (It never occurred to him that the embryo might possibly be female.)

"I will call you Oliver," said Jack to his egg and, hiding it under his bed for the moment, he went outside to see to all his birds.

When he had attended to his budgies, his bantams, and his ducks, he went out into the orchard to see the geese. The four old gray ones raised their heads briefly in greeting and then went on with their grazing, but Lydia and Wilfred came running, beating their white wings and cackling loudly with pleasure. They had long ago learned that Jack kept corn in his pockets, and they nuzzled at him until he fed them.

"Have you laid a second egg, Lydia?" asked Jack, and when the white goose gave a loud honk, he said, "Is that a yes or a no?"

It was a yes, he found, when he looked in the nest in the old shed under the apple tree. And every day for the next week, Lydia laid an egg, until there were nine.

Jack watched her like a hawk.

He had racked his brains to think how he could have the best of both worlds, so that when Lydia went broody, he could fix it for her to hatch her own eggs *and* the ostrich's, but he did not see how it could be done.

If the difference in the incubation periods had been a definite one—thirty days for a goose and thirty-five for an ostrich—he could have removed all of Lydia's as soon as she began to sit, substituted the giant one, and then put the goose eggs back under her five days later. But there was a chance, he knew, that the ostrich egg might take as long as forty-two days, so the goslings might still be out a week too early. There was only one way to ensure the birth of Oliver: all the goose eggs must go.

But Jack was not a farmer's son for nothing. A sitting of fertile goose eggs was worth quite a bit. Nor was he the only farmer's child in his school, and he soon struck a bargain. When, one Saturday morning, Lydia laid the last of her clutch, little did she know that at the other end of the village a couple of broody hens were ready to receive them.

Each morning Jack had gone to the shed early and found Lydia off the nest—and in it one more egg. Now, on Saturday, she did not get off. She

sat tight, looking proud and smug, and allowed Jack, the boy who had a way with birds, to stroke and fondle her, talking to her with honeyed words, while with his other hand he drew, one by one, eight eggs from beneath her and placed them carefully in a large basket. Then he took a great yellowish object from the basket and gently slid it under the sitting bird in place of the ninth and last egg.

"There!" said Jack. "The golden egg that the goose *didn't* lay!" He got to his feet and stood, holding the basket and watching, his heart hammering. Now was the moment for everything to go wrong.

All right, birds could not count, but surely this one would realize that she had been duped, that one egg for nine was not fair exchange but robbery. Now she would forsake the nest and walk away, and Jack's plan would be in ruins.

But with a noise curiously like a sigh of content and a look of great happiness, Lydia settled herself yet more deeply into the warm, downy nest to begin the long incubation of what was to be, for her, a cuckoo child.

5 "Ol-i-ver!"

For the first twenty-four hours, Lydia sat without moving. On Sunday morning the boy came as usual to let them out of the old shed that kept the geese safe from the nighttime fox and, when he had gone, Lydia said, "I must leave the shed."

"Whatever for?" said Wilfred.

As ganders go, he was a handsome fellow, but he was not blessed with a lot of brains.

"I need to go outside," said Lydia.

"Why?" said Wilfred.

"Wilfred," said Lydia patiently, "surely you don't wish me to foul my nest?"

"Oh!" said Wilfred. "Oh, I see! You mean, you want to—"

"Exactly," said Lydia. "I won't be long. Guard the eggs," and she stood up stiffly and waddled out into the orchard.

"Guard the eggs!" said Wilfred to himself. "Of

36

course I will! Why, those eggs are precious, those eggs are priceless, those eggs contain my unborn children! Heaven help anyone who threatens those eggs!" and he walked over and peered proudly into the nest.

Jack had been right—most birds are not too clever at counting, and Wilfred was much less clever than most birds. But even he was a little surprised to see that, instead of "those eggs," the nest contained only one egg, an egg that appeared, even to Wilfred, to be rather on the large side.

He was still staring at it in a vacant sort of way when Lydia reappeared, comfortable now and refreshed from a quick drink and a wash- and brush-up in the duck pond, and proceeded to dig into the mash that the boy had left in the feeding trough.

Wilfred cleared his throat. It would be too strong to say that he was a goose-pecked husband, but he had learned that his wife could be quite sharp with him if he failed to understand any instructions she might give him.

"Lydia, my dear," he said hesitantly.

"What is it?" said Lydia with her beak full.

"You did say, 'Guard the eggs'?"

"I did."

"Well, I don't get it."

"I would have thought," said Lydia, "that it

would have been gosling's play to understand my remark. What is it that confuses you?"

"Look," said Wilfred, gesturing toward the nest.

Lydia looked.

The moment she focused on the giant egg that was the sole occupant of her nest, Lydia reacted in two ways. First, she was surprised. Her arithmetic was not strong (except in comparison to Wilfred's), but she clearly remembered laying a number of eggs. And second, she was determined not to be proved wrong. That would never do. She thought quickly and devised a way out of the problem.

"You see," said Wilfred, "there's only one egg, but you said, 'Guard the eggs.'"

"You misheard me, dear," said Lydia in an affectionate tone of voice. "What I said was, 'Guard the egg, sir.' A respectful way, surely, to address my lord and master?"

"Oh!" said Wilfred. "Oh, yes indeed!" and he walked out into the orchard, happily hissing "Sir! Sir! Sir!" to himself.

Lydia's third reaction, as she surveyed the huge object, was a purely instinctive one. No matter that she did not properly understand what had happened, or how or why the number of eggs that she thought she had been sitting upon had some-

38

how magically fused into a single giant one. No need to worry your head about all that, her instincts told her—just get back on the nest and devote yourself, no matter how long it takes, to brooding this, surely the largest goose egg ever laid, out of which will certainly emerge the largest goose ever known.

Of all the geese in the world, she, Lydia, wife of Wilfred, had been chosen to be the mother of this marvel. Infinitely carefully, the 20-pound bird settled herself upon the egg that could have borne a 280-pound man.

Day followed day and week succeeded week, and Lydia sat tight in the old shed under the apple tree. Twice each day she came off the nest for a short break while Wilfred stood guard.

Wilfred stood guard all day, in fact. He had become used to the size of the egg by now, having nothing to compare it with, and might well have become bored with the whole procedure had not Lydia insisted on his constant presence at her side.

"Your place is here by me," she said, "so you'd better not think you can go gallivanting off with those old gray geese. I am doing all the work. The least you can do is see that I am not disturbed."

So Wilfred was posted as a sentry at the entrance to the shed and ran furiously with outstretched

neck and angry hissings at any hen or duck or turkey that ventured near. He even went after the farm dogs and would no doubt have done the same to a daytime fox should one have come. But luckily this did not happen, and Lydia escaped an early widowhood. As for the humans, Wilfred would not permit Farmer Daw or his wife or Margery (all of whom imagined Lydia to be sitting on a clutch of goose eggs) to enter.

Only Jack was allowed in, partly because he was the bringer of food and partly because, as always, he made them both feel so safe and so special by the touch of his hand and the sound of his voice.

What he said meant nothing to them of course, except for their names. These, by constant repetition, he had taught them, as one would a dog. From the moment of their arrival Jack had addressed each by name every time that he fondled or fed them.

"Wilfred, Wilfred, Wilfred," he would say, stroking the gander's proud (if somewhat empty) head, and "Lydia, Lydia, Lydia," as he smoothed the goose's snowy back, and soon indeed they began to say their names themselves. To a stranger it might have appeared that the two white geese rushing to greet the boy were merely shrieking or cackling, but to Jack it was plain that one was calling out, "Wilfred!" and the other, "Lydia!"

Now, in the old shed under the apple tree, they learned a third name.

Morning and evening, when he came to feed them, Jack would repeat it over and over again, as one would to a parrot. To Wilfred, while Lydia was off exercising, he would say, pointing to the giant egg, "Oliver, Oliver, Oliver." At the same time he would turn it to a different side to prevent the embryo within from sticking to the shell membrane, just in case Lydia was not able to perform this instinctive task herself on so heavy an object. Then, when she came back, he would repeat the new name to her, and it was not long before they knew it by heart.

The slow learner Wilfred indeed took great pride in this new trick, and one day Farmer Daw said to his son, "Funny thing, you know, Jack. If you listen carefully to that noisy white gander of yours, you could swear he was saying 'Oliver.' Listen!"

"I think you're right, Dad," said Jack. "Funny, isn't it?"

And so for forty days and forty nights Lydia bestrode her colossus. Then, very early on the morning of the forty-first day, a Thursday, she felt a movement beneath her. The very smallest of movements it was, but when she rose and bent her head to look, she could see that there was the very smallest of holes in the thick, yellowish shell.

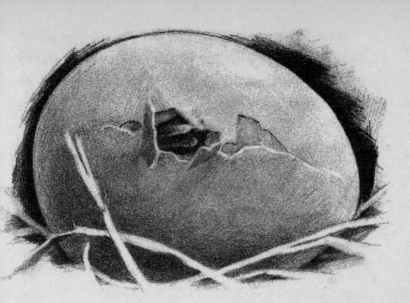

Even as she watched, it grew larger, and within it she could see the tip of a beak. A big beak it seemed, too, and so it should, thought Lydia, for am I not to be the mother of the largest goose ever known?

Jack, too, was awake early that morning and, as usual, the first thing that caught his eye was the calendar hanging by his bed. Forty days had been crossed off, and surely now, he thought anxiously, the ostrich egg will soon hatch. Forty-two days was the maximum incubation period and this was the forty-first, a Thursday. "Thursday's child has far to go" went the old rhyme, but for Lydia and Wilfred, thought Jack, Thursday's child had far to *grow*. If only it hatched safely.

Hastily he began to dress, but even as he stood swaying, one leg in his pants, one out, he heard from the shed in the orchard a loud cacophony of wild, excited sounds.

"Ol-i-ver!" yelled Lydia and Wilfred at the top of their voices. "Ol-i-ver! Ol-i-ver!"

6 The Duck Pond

What exactly Jack had expected to find when he opened the door of the shed he could never afterward remember. As he dashed toward the orchard, his feet jammed hastily into the wrong boots, the hubbub continued unabated.

What had happened? What were they saying? Were those cries for help, because the chick could not break free of the shell? Or were they of horror, at the sight of a child so different? Or were they, as he greatly hoped, of pure joy at a happy hatching?

What would he find in the nest? Would the great egg still be whole, cold by now, a coffin containing the body of a chick that had not had the strength to hatch? Or were the geese shouting encouragement as the baby battled its way into the world? Or had it won the fight, was it even now lying in the ruins of the egg, bedraggled, exhausted, but alive?

What Jack certainly did not expect to see was the scene that greeted him as he flung open the door.

There, standing proudly at attention, like soldiers on parade, were three figures. On the right stood the white gander; on the left the white goose; and between them, upright, bright-eyed, and alert, stood the ostrich chick. So self-assured did he look that it was difficult to believe he had not been around for ages. Only a fragment of eggshell still sticking to his back betrayed his newly hatched status.

"Look at you!" said Jack softly.

Usually at the sound of his voice the geese would shout their own names in reply, but now Lydia and Wilfred bent their heads and with their beaks gently touched the top of the chick's head. Then, with one voice, they softly murmured, "Ol-i-ver," and—the introduction completed—father, mother, and cuckoo child marched smartly out into the morning sunshine. Jack watched them, grinning.

"Oh, Lydia! Oh, Wilfred!" he said. "If you only knew!"

But of course they didn't. They hadn't a clue.

As they walked beside their firstborn, the emotion that filled the white breasts of Lydia and Wilfred was pride. Other geese might hatch out any number of ordinary goslings. But no other geese had such a son as this! Slyly, as they grazed, they watched from the corners of their eyes this wonder child, already pecking at the flowering grass-heads, and marveled at how different he was.

His plumage, for example, was not soft and downy and yellow, but the feathers were spiky, striped orange and black, and the sides of his face and his long neck were spotted with round reddish brown dots like giant freckles. And his legs! How long and strong they already were, with the strangest feet: not for him mere webs, oh no, each of his feet bore two strong toes, and how swiftly he scampered away on them in pursuit of a passing butterfly that had caught his eye, a large brown eye brimming, the geese were sure, with intelligence of the highest order.

But to neither of them did it occur for one moment that Oliver was not of their own kind. To be sure, he was unique; he was not like other goslings, but in the course of time he would grow into the finest goose the world had ever seen. Or rather, the finest gander, for Lydia and Wilfred, no less than Jack, were convinced that they had produced a son.

Now, as they paraded him around the orchard,

all the other poultry came hurrying to inspect the new arrival. The four old gray geese, the hens, the ducks, the turkeys all looked long and hard at Oliver, and then they looked at one another. No one said anything, for no one wished to provoke Wilfred into one of his rages, but the old turkey cock gave a low gobble that sounded suspiciously like laughter. Then they all went away and, once out of earshot, cackled and clucked and quacked and gobbled at one another with amazement and amusement.

"You see!" said Lydia proudly. "They couldn't take their eyes off him!"

"I am not surprised," said Wilfred. "He is so handsome."

"Like his father," said Lydia.

Wilfred nodded his head, pleased, but then a rare thought struck him.

"He doesn't much resemble me," he said. "His color, those legs, the feet. Perhaps he takes after your side of the family, Lydia?"

Before Lydia could answer, a magpie landed on the grass where they stood and, bouncing up toward them jauntily, began to hop around, head cocked to one side, bright eyes examining every detail of the ostrich chick.

"Well, what an odd duck!" said the magpie loudly.

"No," said Wilfred, "he's a goose."

"You could have fooled me, duck," said the magpie.

"No," said Wilfred, "I'm a gander."

"Goodness," said the magpie to Lydia, "your husband's no ordinary Joe!"

"My husband's name," said Lydia severely, "is Wilfred."

"So sue me!" said the magpie.

It hopped closer to Oliver and stood directly in front of him, flirting its long tail up and down.

"What about you, young fellow?" it said. "What do they call you?"

The ostrich chick did not reply. He looked uncertainly up at the geese.

"My son," said Lydia, "is called Oliver. If it is any business of yours. Wilfred, see this impudent bird off!"

"See it off where, dear?" said Wilfred.

"Get rid of it! Attack it! Drive it away!"

The magpie easily avoided Wilfred's clumsy charge and flitted up into an apple tree.

"Oliver! Oliver!" it squawked mockingly. "Ask 'em what sort of bird you are, Oliver!" and it flew away, chattering with merriment.

"What did it mean, Mama?" said Oliver. "You

and me and Papa—we're all the same sort of bird, aren't we?"

"Yes, dear."

"What sort?"

"Geese," said Lydia.

"I'm a geese and you're a geese and Papa's a geese?"

"You can't say 'a geese,'" said Lydia. "Geese means more than one goose. I'm a *goose*."

"So we're three gooses? But Papa told that bird he was a gander?"

"So he is, dear. So are you, a little one."

"But Papa said I was a goose," said Oliver.

"You're a gosling, my boy, and little goslings should be seen and not heard, so shut your beak for a bit," said Wilfred, and he set off for the duck pond, Lydia following.

His brow wrinkled in a frown of puzzlement, the ostrich chick ran to catch up to them, and when they stopped at the rim of the pond and bent their necks for a drink, he copied them.

When they had finished and the surface of the water was once again calm, Oliver looked down and saw in its mirror three more birds. Two of them were obviously the same kind as Mama and Papa; in fact, they looked very much like them. But the third and smallest bird was a really weird-looking creature with spiky orange-and-black striped feathers, standing on long two-toed feet, the sides of its face and its long neck spotted with round reddish brown dots like giant freckles.

"What an object!" thought Oliver, but at that moment all three birds disappeared as Lydia and Wilfred launched themselves into the pond and swam away.

When they reached the middle they looked back to see Oliver still standing at the rim.

"Come on in, son, the water's lovely!" shouted Wilfred, and "Come along, Oliver, dear!" called Lydia.

Gingerly Oliver dipped two toes in and hastily took them out again. "It's wet," he said.

"*You're* wet!" shouted Wilfred. "Come on, son, get in!"

"Swimming's easy, dear," called Lydia. "You'll see."

Still Oliver hesitated, but the duck pond was a large one, and already Mama and Papa seemed a frighteningly long way away, so he shut his eyes and jumped off the rim.

Immediately he found himself in water so deep that only by stretching his neck to its fullest extent could he keep his head out, and a couple of frantic, panic-stricken strides were enough to take that under, too.

"Good boy!" shouted Wilfred from the center of

the pond and, paddling one web only to swing himself to face his wife, he said, "The boy's got spirit after all! For a first dive, that wasn't half bad!"

Lydia did not reply but only watched the surface. "He hasn't come up again," she said.

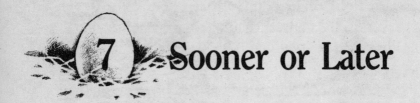

7 Sooner or Later

Jack had been standing outside the shed under the apple tree, watching everything that was going on in the orchard. He saw Oliver being introduced to the rest of the flock of poultry. He saw the magpie fly down and Wilfred drive it away. He saw the family walk toward the duck pond, and not a hint of possible danger crossed his mind, so full was it of other thoughts.

At first, these were all of joy and excitement that he was now the proud owner of a fine specimen of *Struthio camelus,* the camel bird, the largest feathered creature in all the world. Oliver was his!

But even as he said this to himself, he was struck by a much less comfortable thought. The fact that he had taken the egg from the ranger's wheelbarrow had not worried him one bit during all the weeks of its incubation. It would only have been fed to a python. He had saved it from that. That had to be a good thing. But suddenly, as he watched a real, live ostrich chick running about in the orchard, he realized that, technically, Oliver was not his. Oliver belonged to Wildlife Park. Oliver had been stolen. Jack was a thief. That had to be a bad thing.

What would the people at the park say if they knew?

What would his father say when he found out? Would he make him take Oliver back?

Suddenly all these thoughts were shattered by a wild scream from Lydia. Jack, looking up, saw to his horror that Oliver was no longer standing by the rim of the duck pond. There was no sign of him. By the time Jack reached the pond, bubbles were beginning to rise to the surface.

They say that when you are drowning, your whole life flashes before your eyes. If that is so, very old people must take a long time to drown, but though Oliver's past life spanned no more than a quarter of an hour, he was pretty waterlogged by the time Jack hoisted him out. To all intents and purposes, he looked dead.

Jack had learned about first aid in swimming classes at school, but he wasn't too sure about

mouth-to-beak resuscitation, and as for thumping the chick's little chest, that would finish him off if he wasn't already gone.

In fact—and by chance—Jack did the right thing.

First, he sought help. Second, as he ran at top speed for the farmhouse, he carried the chick upside down in one hand, holding it by its legs, its long neck dangling like a bellpull, swinging and jerking about.

So by the time he reached the kitchen, where his mother was preparing breakfast, a lot of the water in Oliver's lungs had drained out.

"Mom! Mom!" shrieked Jack, laying the ostrich chick on the kitchen table. "He fell in the duck pond! I think he's drowned!"

Like all farmers, Mrs. Daw was used to dealing with animal emergencies. She did not waste time asking questions but picked up the chick and felt its bedraggled body.

"His heart's beating," she said, "but he's cold and in shock." She quickly wrapped him in a towel. Only his head stuck out, the eyes closed, but as Jack and his mother watched, Oliver gave a feeble sputter. Then he spit up some more pond water.

"He'll be all right," said Jack's mother. "Funny thing, but it takes a long time for young creatures to drown. That's why it's so cruel when people drown kittens. Now then, into the oven with him. Open the door of the bottom oven, Jack," and when Jack did so, she put the wrapped chick on the lowest shelf.

"Watch him," she said. "I must get on with breakfast."

Jack knelt by the open oven door, praying for Oliver to open his eyes and, in a minute or so, he did. Already, Jack noticed, he had lovely long eyelashes. Then the chick made a funny little sound, part chirp, part croak, part belch. To anyone else it would have been just a noise. To Jack, who had a way with birds, it was no problem to translate.

Oliver was saying, "Thank you."

By the time Jack's father had come hungrily in from his shed and Margery had come sleepily down from her bedroom for breakfast, Oliver had been restored to health. Ten minutes in the low oven, then a gentle toweling from Jack, and finally, a teaspoonful of cooking sherry from Jack's mother, had made a new chick of him, and he was walking, albeit a little shakily, across the kitchen floor.

"Do we have to have one of Jack's beastly birds running around when we're eating?" grumbled Margery.

"He fell in the duck pond," said her mother. "We've just been drying him out."

"His name is Oliver," said Jack.

Jack's father picked up the chick in his large farmer's hands.

"So you've been a taking a bath, Oliver?" he said. "Doesn't look to me as though you're any kind of waterfowl, not with feet like that."

He examined one of Oliver's strange two-toed feet and looked at the length of his legs and of his

neck and at his odd freckled markings. Then he gave him to Jack to hold.

"I've seen a few chicks of one sort or another in my time," said Farmer Daw, "but never one like this fellow."

"I haven't asked you, Jack," said Mrs. Daw, "because I knew your father would. But now I think you'd better tell us. What is it?"

Gently Jack stroked Oliver's back, dry and warm again now.

"It's an ostrich," he said.

"An ostrich?" cried Margery. "Oh, you are such a liar, Jack!"

"I'm not," said Jack. "I got an ostrich egg from Wildlife Park when my class went on that trip, and I set it under Lydia, and she hatched it this morning."

"Wait a minute," said his father. "You say you got an ostrich egg. How did you get it?"

"Were you given it?" asked his mother.

"No."

"Did you buy it?" asked his father.

"No."

"You stole it!" cried Margery. "Oh, you're a little thief, Jack! You stole it, didn't you?"

"Yes," said Jack. "I did."

"Eat your breakfast, both of you," said Mrs. Daw

to her husband and daughter. To her son she said, "You'd better tell us all about it."

So Jack told them the whole story, from the moment when he had first set eyes on the magnificent black-and-white bird, half as tall again as a man, one of whose chicks he now held in his arms.

When he had finished there was a moment's silence.

Then, "You'll have to take him back," said Farmer Daw.

"Oh, Dad," said Jack quietly. "Not yet!"

"Of course you will," said Margery. "He doesn't belong to you. He belongs to Wildlife Park. You stole him."

"I didn't steal *him,*" said Jack. "I stole an egg that was going to be fed to a snake. Nobody wanted it. It might not even have been fertile, for all I knew. If it hadn't been for me, Oliver wouldn't have been born, and if it hadn't been for me, he'd have been drowned by now," and he hugged the ostrich chick to him, blinking away the threat of tears.

Margery opened her mouth for a further taunt, but her mother silenced her with a fierce frown and a shake of the head. She caught her husband's eye and made, to him, a very different face, eyebrows raised, head a little to one side, with the hint of a smile.

Farmer Daw swallowed his last mouthful and pushed his chair back from the table.

"We'll have to think about this, Jack," he said. "Stealing is stealing, however you dress it up. And anyway, imagine having an ostrich on the farm! Whoever heard of such a thing!" He grinned despite himself. "He'll have to go back," he said. "Sooner or later."

"Later, Dad," said Jack. "Please!"

His father hesitated in the kitchen doorway. Through the open door they could all hear a doleful duet coming from the orchard.

"Ol-i-ver! Ol-i-ver!" cried Lydia and Wilfred, thinking they were in mourning for their lost child.

"Oh, go on then," said Farmer Daw. "Put him back with them. But only for the time being, remember."

"Yes, Dad! Thanks, Dad!" said Jack, and he ran for the orchard, carrying Oliver, this time rightside up.

8) The Most Marvelous Goose

"Oliver darling!" cried Lydia. "Oh, my poor baby! Are you all right?"

"Yes, thank you, Mama," said Oliver.

"Oh, I will never forget it as long as I live!" said Lydia. "That terrible moment when you didn't come up again! It was the mud, I suppose. You got your feet stuck in the mud, that must have been it. Nasty, sticky stuff. It's those dirty ducks; they make it so mucky. You mustn't go in that pond again till you're much bigger."

"No, Mama," said Oliver. "I won't."

"There's a good gosling," said Lydia. "Oh, Oliver, I can't tell you what it's been like! We've been out of our minds with worry, your father and I, haven't we, Wilfred?"

Wilfred did not answer. The truth was, he had not so much been out of what little mind he had with worry as he was filled with a mixture of disappointment and scorn. Coming as he did from a proud line of waterfowl, for whom swimming was as natural as walking (and more gracefully performed at that), he found it very hard to stomach the bitter fact that a son of his had simply sunk.

Stuck in the mud—my web! he thought. The boy had panicked. Like many stupid folk, Wilfred was brave purely because he had never known the meaning of fear, and to suspect his son of being a coward was agony. But that's what he is, he said to himself. The boy's chicken! His thoughts were interrupted by the sound of his wife's voice.

"Wilfred!" she said sharply. "I asked you a question. Well?"

Sometimes, if Wilfred had not listened to or, more likely, had not understood Lydia's questions, he would take an even-money gamble and answer either yes or no. But this could earn him a sharp talking-to if he guessed wrong, so he had devised a slightly safer method.

"I quite agree, my dear," he said.

"You see," said Lydia to Oliver. "Papa was worried stiff, too."

And still is, thought Wilfred. "Oliver, boy," he said.

"Yes, Papa?"

"*Why* did you sink?"

"Wilfred!" cried Lydia. "Do you listen to *nothing* I say? I told you, he got his feet stuck in the mud, didn't you, Oliver?"

"No, Mama," said Oliver. He turned to face the gander.

"It's quite simple, Papa," he said. "I sank because I cannot swim."

There was a silence as the two geese digested this remark in different ways.

Wilfred suddenly felt much happier. It looked as though the boy might not be chicken after all. In fact, thought Wilfred, if he jumped in knowing he could not swim, that was a brave thing to do! (For Wilfred *brave* and *foolhardy* were one and the same.) What it all meant was that here was a gosling who, for some as yet unexplained reason, had not learned to swim.

"Don't worry, boy!" he shouted. "I'll soon teach you!"

"Wilfred!" said Lydia angrily. "You heard me tell Oliver that he is not to go into that pond until he is much bigger. Perhaps you will be good enough in the future not to contradict, contravene, gainsay, or generally run counter to my express instructions!"

Puzzled by his wife's language but warned by the tone of her voice, Wilfred played it safe.

"I quite agree, my dear," he said.

Lydia's reaction to hearing the ostrich chick say that he could not swim had been very different. A degree of logical thought—something denied Wilfred—was within her grasp, and it went as follows:

All geese can swim.

Oliver cannot swim.

Therefore Oliver is not a goose.

For the first time a shadow of doubt concerning her child crossed Lydia's mind. Admittedly she had never had a gosling of her own before, but she had been one herself not all that long ago, and she could clearly remember, thinking about it now, what her brothers and sisters had looked like. And they had not looked at all like Oliver.

So what is he? Of what, she asked herself perplexedly, am I the mother?

For an instant she considered sharing her doubts with her husband but just as quickly rejected the idea. Just supposing Oliver were not a goose, Wilfred would still consider him one even if he grew nine feet tall! As for me, she said to herself, I don't care. He's alive and safe and beautiful, and he's my son!

"Come along, Oliver darling," she said. "The boy is bringing your breakfast now. You must eat up every scrap and then you'll grow up to be big and strong. Why, who knows, one day you might even be bigger than Papa, isn't that right, Wilfred?"

Wilfred, who hadn't listened to a word, said, "I quite agree, my dear."

How Jack, watching, would have laughed if he could have understood Lydia's last remark. He could of course interpret a certain amount of goose speech—shouts of welcome, cries of alarm, companionable chucklings and honkings and mutterings, angry noises when Wilfred lost his temper with a dog or the turkey cock or when Lydia lost her temper with Wilfred—and now Jack prepared to try to fathom the rudiments of ostrich language.

As the days passed, Jack became aware of one particular sound that Oliver made almost constantly as he foraged in the orchard with his foster parents. It was a shrill, thin whistle. There was never any difficulty in finding where Oliver was. You could hear him whistling.

At first Jack worried about this, thinking it might be some kind of distress call, until one day he found, in the public library, a large modern reference book on birds. It had much more to say about ostriches than his old edition of *Birds of the World,* and it explained the noise.

"Often," it said, "a number of broods of ostrich chicks of much the same age will band together in one flock of as many as forty or fifty individuals. Contact between these chicks, as they search for food among the tall grass, is maintained by sound, each chick keeping up a constant whistling."

The book also described the call of the adult male ostrich: "a hollow, booming noise, used as an alarm or as a threat; this *boom* is very like the distant roar of a lion but without the finishing grunt."

At about a month old, Oliver began to give up whistling, presumably because there was no one to whistle back at him, but by then he was making three other noises that Jack could clearly distinguish.

The first was *"boo!"*—not the jeering, sneering boo of an angry football fan but a short, sudden noise such as one might make on jumping out from hiding to frighten someone.

The second was *"twoo!"* This was a softer, long, drawn-out sound, not melancholy like an owl's hoot but on a gentle, happy note.

The third was *"hrup!"*—the noise of a man clearing his throat.

"Boo!" Jack learned, was used as a greeting ("hello!" or "good morning!" or "nice to see you!")

or as a summons ("come and see what I've found, Mama" or "hurry up with my breakfast").

"Twoo!" meant happiness, pleasure at being stroked and petted, delight at finding a fat worm, or the simple joy of running about in the sunshine on ever-lengthening legs.

The meaning of *"hrup!"* was made plain to Jack one morning when he had scattered a handful of chick feed on the grass for Oliver. This was a useful way of feeding the ostrich chick, for Lydia and Wilfred were clumsy at picking up these crumbs, allowing Oliver the lion's share. But, as Jack watched, one of his bantam hens came running up to steal food from under the ostrich's very beak.

"Hrup!" said Oliver loudly, and he gave the little bird a hefty kick that sent it scuttling away in squawking fright.

And so the weeks passed, and with them Jack's fear grew. For how much longer would he be allowed to keep his unusual pet?

"He'll have to go back," Father had said. "Sooner or later."

How soon was later?

Jack's fear was not, however, the only thing that was growing. So was his family's affection for the ostrich chick.

To the farmer, the sight of a healthy, thriving animal of any sort was a pleasure, and this exotic creature particularly took his fancy.

Mrs. Daw—perhaps because of her part in the rescue from the duck pond, perhaps from a feeling similar to Lydia's obvious maternal pride—found that she had a very soft spot for Jack's pet.

And even Margery, who normally took no notice of any of her brother's birds, had (though she would never have admitted it to Jack) come under Oliver's spell: he had come running to her one day as she crossed the orchard and had serenaded her with so warm and full-throated a *twoo!* that she really fell for him.

Fastest growing of all, of course, was not Jack's worry or the family's liking, but Oliver himself.

At birth he had been a foot tall. Now, at six months of age, he was three times that height, towering over Lydia and Wilfred. And how, indeed, they looked up to him!

Lydia, though she did not know (and would never know) what he was, knew without doubt that her amazing child was the most marvelous creature.

Wilfred thought him the most marvelous goose. He had accepted the fact that Oliver could not swim or (so far as he knew) fly. But what filled him with pride was the speed of the boy! At about four weeks old, Oliver had begun to run really fast, startling the old gray geese and the hens and the ducks and the turkeys as he flashed by them. But now he had shifted into high gear.

"The ostrich is capable of speeds of between 30 and 40 mph," said the bird book, and for slowpoke Wilfred it was sheer delight to watch his sprinting son.

"Look at him!" he shouted at Lydia one morning as Oliver hurtled by with the speed of a galloping horse. "There's never been a goose like that!"

To which Lydia, with a wry cackle, replied, "I quite agree, my dear."

Jack and his father were watching, too.

"Look at him!" said Farmer Daw. "How much bigger is he going to grow?"

"It says in the books, four feet high at one year of age, and eight feet or more when fully grown," said Jack. "Some are nine feet."

"Nine feet! That's half as tall again as me! He won't fit in that shed under the apple tree then."

Jack swallowed. "He won't be here then, Dad, will he?"

"Well, no, I suppose not."

"You said he'll have to go back to the park."

"Well, yes."

"When?"

At that moment Oliver drew up before them, scarcely out of breath. He stared at them with his large brown eyes and fluttered his long, long lashes.

"Boo!" he said politely and, stretching out his serpentine neck, offered to each in turn the top of his head for a scratch, something he particularly enjoyed.

"Twoo!" said Oliver softly to the father. *"Twoo!"* he said to the son.

Jack sighed deeply. "Dad," he said, "when *will* he have to go back?"

Farmer Daw grinned a bit sheepishly. "Oh, sooner or later," he said.

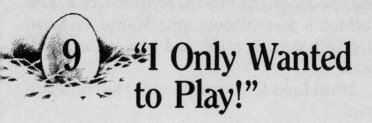

9 "I Only Wanted to Play!"

On his first birthday, Oliver hit the roof.

For some time now he had towered above his foster parents, but that morning when Jack opened the door of the old shed under the apple tree, he saw that the top of Oliver's head was actually touching the tin roof.

"Happy birthday, dear Oliver, happy birthday to you!" sang Jack, a little sadly. Then he added, "For I don't suppose I'll sing it again next year—you'll be gone."

He fed the family and then he went and borrowed a ruler from his father's workshop and measured the inside height of the shed. Four feet—just as the books had said.

Jack folded the ruler and was just about to go out when he saw, in the darkest corner of the shed, a nest—and, in it, a goose egg!

Before very many days had passed, Lydia completed her clutch and was sitting, and a month after that she hatched eight goslings.

How thrilled everyone was when she first marched them out into the orchard! Jack was delighted, it goes without saying. Wilfred was bursting with fatherly pride. And how excited Oliver was!

When Lydia first began to sit, he had been puzzled.

"Aren't you coming out with us, Mama?" he said, bending his long neck and fluttering his long eyelashes at her.

"No, dear," said Lydia. "I'm just going to sit here for a while."

Oliver ran to find Wilfred.

"Boo!" he said, and then, as he strode beside the gander very slowly, to keep pace, "Papa, what's the matter with Mama?"

"Matter?" said Wilfred. "Nothing's the matter, son. You'll soon have lots of brothers and sisters. Your mother's going to have a lot of babies, that's what she's going to do."

"Oh," said Oliver. He had forgotten his own birth and he was pretty vague about the whole business.

"Baby whats?" he said.

"Baby goslings, of course."

"Like me?"

76

Wilfred raised his head from the grass and looked up at the young ostrich. For some months now he had taken Oliver rather for granted, not really noticing the changes in him. Now he stared up and saw a four-foot-high young giant, quite different in coloring: gone were the reddish brown dots from face and neck, and the spiky orange-and-black striped feathers had softened and darkened—except for the wing and tail plumes, which were white. How long his neck is, too, thought Wilfred; and his legs, how muscular they are. His glance, traveling downward, fell upon those huge two-toed feet.

"She's going to have goslings like me?" asked Oliver again.

Wilfred shook his head violently, as though to clear his thoughts. "No," he said. "They will not be like you are now, because you have grown big. You are not a gosling anymore."

"What am I, then?"

"You are a gander," said Wilfred. "Like me."

They walked forward to the rim of the pond that, thirteen months before, had nearly been the death of Oliver, and stood, looking at their reflections in the water.

"Like you?" said Oliver doubtfully.

But he forgot his doubts when he first saw his eight little brothers and sisters. He could think

only how pretty they were as they toddled along in single file behind Lydia.

"Twoo! Twoo!" he cried, and he cantered toward them, eager for a game with these new playmates.

Mercifully, he did not step on any of them, but several were tipped over by the ostrich's huge feet and lay helplessly on their backs, paddling their little webs in the air and peeping with fright.

Furious at his clumsiness, Lydia flew at him, buffeting him with her wings, and, as he turned away, an equally angry Wilfred came hissing at him and biting at his legs.

"Mama! Papa!" cried Oliver in distress. "I only wanted to play!" but the two white geese were already hustling the goslings away. Straight to the duck pond they went and, as Oliver watched, the memory of his own first (and almost last) day of life flashed into his horrified mind. If there had been sand about, perhaps he would have buried his head in it, but as it was, he could only shut his eyes. But when at last he opened them again, it was to see the eight goslings swimming easily and happily about with their parents.

Jack, who had been watching all this, now came up and put an arm around Oliver's long neck.

"Poor Oliver!" he said. "It's hard for you to understand, isn't it?"

"Hrup!" said Oliver, not in anger but in sorrow. He turned his head at right angles, a trick he had, to look directly at Jack, and his great brown eyes, the boy could see, were full of sadness.

"I'm afraid you're just going to have to get used to it," said Jack. "Lydia and Wilfred are bound to be pretty wrapped up in these new babies. You're going to have to take a backseat. But you're my favorite, you know that, don't you?"

He scratched the top of the ostrich's head, now almost level with his own, and Oliver managed a faint *"Twoo."*

"Just be careful where you put your big feet," said Jack.

"Just be careful where you put your big feet," said

79

Wilfred sharply when he and Lydia returned with the goslings.

"Yes, Papa," said Oliver.

Lydia, seeing him look so woebegone, spoke in kinder tones.

"Better still, be a good goose and don't move till we're safely past you, Oliver dear," she said.

"Yes, Mama," said Oliver. He stood motionless until the file of goslings began to pass him, but then he couldn't resist stretching his neck down until his head was on a level with theirs.

"Awfully sorry I knocked you over," he said, as quietly as he could, but the goslings all stampeded wildly, peeping with fright.

But that wasn't the worst.

At twilight the white geese and their eight new children headed for the safety and shelter of the old shed, but Oliver found his way barred. Wilfred stood in the entrance.

"Sorry, boy," he said gruffly. "You'll have to bed down somewhere else. Your mother's frightened you'll tread on the goslings, and the goslings are frightened of you. You're too big."

At that moment Jack arrived on his evening rounds, shutting up all the different poultry in all the different sheds and houses to be safe from the fox.

He saw at once what was happening.

"Inside, Wilfred," he said, and Wilfred obeyed, and Jack shut the door. "Come along, Oliver," he said. "We'll find you a place of your very own and get you something special for supper."

The place turned out to be an old stable, where horses had lived in the days before tractors, and where there was plenty of space and headroom. The supper was a large apple.

As a little chick, Oliver had pecked at and swallowed grass, beetles, worms, wood lice—anything edible. Each bit of food had gone straight down. But now, nearly adult, he had begun to eat as grown-up ostriches do, retaining food in his mouth until there was enough to form quite a large ball, or bolus, which he would then swallow, so that an onlooker could see the spherical shape traveling slowly down Oliver's throat.

Jack stood for a moment, watching the apple descend, and then, after a final scratch on the top of Oliver's head, he bolted the stable door.

Oliver got little sleep that night. For hours, he padded up and down the length of the cobbled stable floor, feeling extremely sorry for himself. True, the boy had been nice to him, as always, but Mama and Papa had not only attacked him but also turned him away from his home, from his birthplace. "It's not fair!" said Oliver. "*Hrup!* It's just not fair!" and in his frustration he kicked

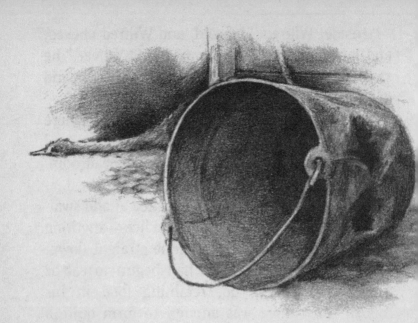

out, with one of his sharp-clawed two-toed feet, at a bucket that stood on the floor and sent it spinning across the stable. At last, tired out, he folded his long legs beneath him and sank to the floor, neck outstretched and chin resting on the cobblestones, and he slept.

Oliver got to his feet when Jack came to let him out, but his spirits did not rise. Lydia and Wilfred, so preoccupied were they with the goslings, took only the barest notice of his greeting *boo!* and would shout a warning "Ol-i-ver!" each time he approached too closely.

Jack, watching, worried. Just why a sturdy bucket in the stable had two gaping holes torn in it he did not know, but he did know that Oliver was unhappy—and why.

He's been rejected by his family, Jack thought. But of course, they're not really his family. He should be with his own kind. Oh, I don't want to lose him, the last thing I want is to lose him, but perhaps it's time for him to go back to Wildlife Park.

For days Jack agonized about this, but then, when the goslings were a couple of weeks old, something happened that was to postpone any such decision.

It was a sunny Sunday morning, and though there is no day of rest for a farming family, the Daws were taking it easy. Mr. and Mrs. Daw were looking through the papers, Margery was reading a novel, and Jack was deep in *Birds of the World*.

Out in the orchard, the various poultry cackled and clucked and quacked and gobbled, enjoying the warmth without a care in the world.

Lydia and Wilfred grazed side by side, their minds, now that their children were older, not so constantly on them. They had not noticed in fact that the eight goslings, busily hunting among the grasses for insects, had strayed toward the far end of the orchard. It was bounded there by a stone wall, beyond which was a forest.

As the goslings neared the wall, they suddenly saw that, lying flat upon the top of it, was an animal. To their innocent eyes it looked something like one of the farm dogs, to which they were already accustomed, knowing they would do the birds no harm. To be sure, the farm dogs were black-and-white, and this little dog was a fiery russet red, but that meant nothing to the goslings. Peeping and chirping to one another, they wandered closer. On the wall the fox lay, almost as still as a statue. The only movement it made was to lick its lips.

10 "BOOM!"

The fox was an old one, full of wisdom. A night hunter like all his kind, he was nonetheless a specialist in daytime raids. He had planned this one carefully.

A few days earlier he had slipped down from his earth in a distant hillside to have a good look at the lay of the land. Behind the buildings of the farm, he had found there was an orchard filled with a variety of poultry, and at the far eastern end of the orchard was a forest.

Behind the stone wall at the woods' edge he had paused and tested the breeze with his sharp nose. The prevailing west wind brought him a medley of farmyard smells, many of them mouth-watering; but on that particular morning one of the farm collies had chanced to be crossing the orchard, and at the scent of it the fox had melted back into the woods.

Now he had once again come in upwind, and this time he found nothing to worry about, for the dogs were asleep at Farmer Daw's feet as he read the Sunday papers.

The old fox had lain luxuriously on top of the wall, savoring the delicious aroma of hen and duck and goose and turkey and watching the eight goslings draw near. Beyond them he could see poultry of every size and shape, including one bird that was unfamiliar to him as it stood by itself on ridiculously long legs.

A gosling, the fox thought, is not much more than a mouthful, but I'll pull off their silly little heads before I get myself something more substantial. One of those two white geese, for example—that'd be worth taking home. He licked his lips.

So confident was the fox of there being plenty of time to go about his butchery undisturbed that he stood up and stretched prior to jumping down from the wall. The movement was seen by the sharpest pair of eyes in the orchard.

Oliver had been standing by himself, wanting to go and forage beside his little brothers and sisters, but not daring to for fear of being scolded.

At least I can look at them, he thought, there can't be any harm in that, and he stared at the eight distant shapes with those great eyes whose keen sight give the ostrich, on its native African plains, early warning of any far-off enemy. What kind of animal it was that now dropped from the stone wall he did not know, but it looked unusual and interesting.

"Boo!" said Oliver loudly, and at the sound Lydia looked up from her grazing and saw the fox.

"Children!" she shrieked. "Come to Mama! Run quickly!" and the goslings, startled, scuttled to obey.

Behind them padded the self-assured raider, in no hurry, enjoying the little victims' panic, content to play cat and mouse with them, particularly as the two foolish white geese were now rushing directly toward him, aiming, it seemed, to run down his throat!

Wildly Lydia and Wilfred beat their wings as they hastened, screeching, across the grass in a gallant attempt at rescue that could only have ended in death for the whole family. But while they were still fifty yards away and the fox was but a few feet from the hindmost of the madly fleeing goslings, a tall figure shot past the hurrying geese. Oliver might have been only half grown but already he could run at full speed, the amazing speed of *Struthio camelus,* the camel bird, and as he passed Lydia and Wilfred, they might as well have been standing still. His little brothers and sisters were in mortal danger—that he knew from their panic-stricken cries and from the anguished voices of his mother and father—and as he ran, there burst from him in anger his first-ever adult sound, a "booming noise . . . like the distant roar of a lion."

"BOOM!" bellowed Oliver as he raced to the rescue at forty miles an hour.

At the sound the old fox, his jaws already agape to fasten on the slowest gosling, hesitated for a second, but in that second one life was saved and another lost. A last bound took Oliver clear over the goslings' heads, and as he landed in front of the snarling fox he lashed out with one mighty kick that sent a fiery russet red shape whirling and twirling into the air to fall flat, twitch twice, and lie limp.

Oliver stood beside the lifeless foe, his wings and plumed tail raised and his head held high, and danced a short victory dance.

"BOOM!" he roared once more.

Then the fire died out of his great eyes, his wings dropped to his side, and he lowered his head as Lydia and Wilfred arrived upon the scene, breathless from running and from sheer amazement. Behind them trailed the eight goslings, wide-eyed with wonder; they did not understand what had been happening, but they dimly realized that this enormous brother of theirs—of whom they had

all been so scared—had saved their lives. Nervously, the boldest of them made his way forward to stand by the ostrich's feet and, tipping his little head right back, peeped a message of thanks on behalf of them all.

"Twoo!" said Oliver very softly, and he bent his head to the ground and gently touched beaks with his sibling.

Lydia and Wilfred stood side by side, looking at the dead fox.

"Oliver darling," said Lydia, "you were wonderful."

"Good boy, Oliver!" said Wilfred in his heartiest voice. "I'm proud of you, my son! A gander killing a fox! Imagine that!"

"I shouldn't, if I were you," said Lydia dryly. She looked at those great two-toed feet, around which the goslings, their fear of their big brother gone, were happily waddling on their little webs. Once again a piece of logic occurred to her:

All geese have webbed feet.

Oliver does not have webbed feet.

Therefore Oliver is not a goose.

And thank goodness he's not, she thought. If it weren't for him we would all be dead, and so would many of the other birds, too, I dare say. She looked down the orchard to see the old gray geese and

90

the hens and ducks and turkeys, all of which had fled at the sight of the fox, cautiously returning.

And through them now came the Daw family, running.

At the first *BOOM!* Jack, who knew immediately the origin of that noise, threw down *Birds of the World* and dashed out, calling the dogs. The others followed as the second *BOOM!* sounded.

Now they reached the scene, breathless from running and from sheer amazement, and gazed down at the body lying in the grass, while the collies sniffed, with low growls and raised hackles, at the two gaping holes torn in its side. Jack, watching, recalled the stable bucket.

"What. . . ?" began Margery.

"How. . . ?" said Mrs. Daw.

"Who. . . ?" said Farmer Daw.

"Oliver," said Jack. "A kick from a full-grown ostrich can kill a man, the ranger at the wildlife park told us, so a kick from a half-grown one can kill a fox. Oliver has saved the goslings' lives!"

"And a lot more lives besides," said his father. "You know what a fox is like—as long as anything flutters in front of him, he'll kill it. There would have been a massacre here this morning if it weren't for your Oliver, Jack."

"Oh, Oliver!" said Jack. "You're a hero!"

To which the ostrich replied, *"Twoo! Twoo!"*

"Sounds like he's saying 'Too true!' " laughed Jack's mother. "Ah well, time I started lunch."

Farmer Daw looked down at the dead fox, the brightness of its red coat already seemingly faded.

"No more Sunday lunches for you, you old devil," he said, and he picked the animal up by the tail.

"One of you children fetch a shovel," he said.

By the time Farmer Daw had finished digging a hole, most of the orchard's inhabitants had already forgotten the morning's drama, though the goslings had had to listen to a stern lecture from Lydia.

"You are never," she had ended, "to stray away by yourselves like that again, do you understand? Mama is very angry with you!"

Wilfred, reckoning that what was good for the goose was good for the gander, added, "And Papa is very angry, too. You must do as Mama says, or you will never grow up to be big geese."

"Like Oliver?" said one of the goslings.

Wilfred hesitated, confused, but Lydia said briskly, "Now come along, all of you, follow me," and off they went.

Only Oliver stood by the hole at Jack's side, watching gravely as the farmer tipped the body of the fox into it and began to shovel back the earth.

So intent was the burial party on the business at hand that nobody noticed a blue-uniformed figure entering the orchard and walking, with steps that were noiseless on the turf, toward them.

"Dad," said Jack, as his father thumped the little mound of earth with the flat of the shovel. "We can't send him back now. Not after what he's done."

Farmer Daw sighed. "I don't rightly know what to do," he said. "Trouble is, you can't just forget how he came to be here, you know. That egg he came out of was not your property. You stole it. You may not like it, Jack, but the fact remains— you're a thief."

"Hello," said a voice behind them, and man, boy, and ostrich turned to see the local police sergeant.

"What's all this then, Mr. Daw?" he said. "You say your son's a thief?"

11 A Lump in the Throat

"And before you answer that," said the sergeant, "what in the world's that thing standing by you?"

He stared quizzically at Oliver, and Oliver fluttered his eyelashes at him and uttered a quiet, polite *boo!*

"Fierce, is it?" said the sergeant to Jack.

But before he could answer, his father said, "No, he wouldn't say 'boo' to a goose."

This was so far from the truth—for every morning Oliver greeted his foster parents in this very fashion—that Jack had to stifle a giggle, despite the seriousness of the situation. But then his spirits fell.

It was all over now. The policeman would report him to the director of the wildlife park, and Oliver would have to go back there, and Jack would probably go to prison for stealing the egg. Better make a clean breast of it, now, he thought. It might count in my favor.

"Please," he said, "it's my ostrich, I mean, it's an ostrich, and his name is Oliver, and he's saved the lives of all our poultry by killing a fox that we were just burying here, and one of my geese hatched him out of an egg" (he paused for breath) "that I stole from the wildlife park."

The police sergeant took off his helmet and scratched the top of his head thoughtfully.

Jack scratched the top of Oliver's nervously.

"I don't know, I'm sure," said the sergeant. "I just came out here to get your dad to buy a couple of raffle tickets to benefit the Police Benevolent Fund, and what do I find? A dead body, a bird that's a murderer, and a boy that's guilty of larceny. And I shouldn't be surprised if there weren't other offenses to be taken into consideration. You may need a license to keep an ostrich. And third-party insurance, I wouldn't be surprised. And how about the Wild Birds Protection Act? Taking the eggs of a rare bird, as I remember, carries a fine of fifty dollars or a month's imprisonment, for a first offense."

Jack looked so downcast at this that the police sergeant, a kind man, hastened to reassure him. "I'm joking," he said. "Don't worry—I'm not going to say anything about your precious ostrich. That's up to your dad to sort out. I'll keep my mouth shut—on one condition."

"What's that?" asked Jack fearfully.

"That your father buys a whole book of these raffle tickets."

"Thanks, sergeant," said Farmer Daw. "I'll certainly do that. And look, don't you worry either, we're going to put this matter right—with the wildlife park, I mean."

"It's just as well, Mr. Daw," said the police sergeant. "I know you're pretty isolated here, and this orchard's tucked away around the back, but sooner or later someone's going to set eyes on this fellow and then you'll have the press here and the television crews and Lord knows what. Imagine having an ostrich on the farm! Who ever heard of such a thing?"

"What are we going to do, Dad?" said Jack when the policeman had gone.

"We're going to drive over to the park this very afternoon, you and I, and we're going to see the director, and you're going to tell him everything. Better make a clean breast of it now; it might count in your favor."

Jack ate very little of that Sunday lunch. He felt sick. Owning up to something bad that you've done is always difficult, and now he must not only own up and be punished, but he would lose Oliver, too. One day, he had been telling himself for a long while now, Oliver would have to go, but now that day was almost here. Tomorrow, probably, they would come for him with a van or a truck and cart him off. Just when he's become a hero, thought Jack—to my family and to his.

He ran to the orchard gate while his father was getting the car out and looked over.

There were Lydia and Wilfred, paddling placidly on the pond, enjoying each other's company, free for the moment from the trials of parenthood.

The goslings were safe and happy, they knew, in the charge of their baby-sitter, who was taking them for a walk.

Oliver took one slow pace to twenty of each of his siblings', terribly careful of where he was putting his big feet, while the eight goslings scuttered merrily about, pipping and peeping at their giant brother.

Oliver looked up and saw Jack.

"Boo!" he said cheerily and then returned to duty, with many a soft *twoo!* to his little charges and one loud *hrup!* when the turkey cock approached too closely.

All the way to the wildlife park Jack tried to convince himself that the director would be as nice as the police sergeant had been. The sergeant had been large and stout, and his round, clean-shaven face had broken easily into a smile. He looked like a friendly bear.

But when they were admitted to the director's office, he wasn't a bit like that. He was small and thin, with a narrow face and a ginger beard. In fact, he reminded Jack of the late fox.

"Mr. . . . Daw, is it?" he said to Jack's father. "What can I do for you?"

Farmer Daw put his hand on Jack's shoulder and gave it a reassuring squeeze. "This is my boy, Jack," he said. "He has something to tell you."

"Yes?" said the director.

Jack tried hard to keep his voice steady but all the same it trembled as he said, "I stole one of your ostrich eggs."

Slowly the director lifted a paw and pulled at his ginger beard. His face wore so foxy a look that Jack began to feel like a helpless gosling.

"How?" said the director softly.

"It was last year," said Jack. "I came here on a school trip. The ranger was showing us some os- trich eggs—spare ones that he was going to feed to the snakes—and I stole one."

"You are an egg collector?" said the director, a snarl in his voice.

"No!" said Jack. "No, I think taking birds' eggs

98

just to put them in a glass case is an awful thing to do. No, I wanted to try to hatch it."

"He's crazy about birds," put in Jack's father. "He has a way with them."

"Just a moment, Mr. Daw," said the director. "Let me get this straight." To Jack he said, "You didn't, of course."

"Didn't what?"

"Didn't succeed in hatching it?"

"Yes," said Jack, "I did. Well, one of my geese did. I call him Oliver. He's a year old now—nearly a year and a quarter."

"He?" said the director. "How do you know it's a cock?"

"Well, I didn't, really, when he was little," said

99

Jack. "I just had a feeling he was. But lately his feathers have darkened a lot. Another few months and I reckon he'll be black-and-white. And he's started to *boom*. It sounds just like the book said it would."

"And how was that?"

"Like the distant roar of a lion but without the finishing grunt."

"Quite the expert, aren't we?" said the director. A cunning look came into his foxy eyes.

"So you're telling me," he said, "that you are the owner of a specimen of the African Somali ostrich, *Struthio molybdophanes?*"

"No," said Jack. "Oliver is a North African ostrich, *Struthio camelus.*"

" 'Strewth!" said the director. Just for a moment he looked more human than vulpine.

"The point is," said Farmer Daw, "that Jack is not the owner. He took the egg, and so the bird that hatched from it is not his property but yours. I'll give you my address and then you'd better collect it."

The director pulled again at his ginger beard. "I'll come and have a look at him," he said.

"When?" said Jack.

"Tomorrow."

"Tomorrow," said Jack to Oliver in the stable that

evening. Lydia and Wilfred had been pestered by the goslings to allow their big brother to sleep in the old shed with them, but Jack had not thought it a good idea: apart from the hazard of his big feet, Oliver had grown another six inches.

"Tomorrow they're going to come and take you away from me."

Oliver turned his head and gazed into Jack's eyes, puzzled perhaps by his sad tone. Jack scratched the top of the ostrich's head. Probably for the last time, he thought. There was a lump in his throat.

There was a lump in Oliver's throat, too—his supper.

Jack watched as the bolus, the size of a baseball, slipped slowly down the ostrich's neck, and his spirits fell with it.

When he awoke the next day, Jack wished, for the first time in his life, that he was going to school that Monday morning. It was cowardly, he knew, but that way he would miss all of it—the last good-byes, the sight of Oliver being caught (by the rangers that the director would bring with him) with a net that probably would frighten him and then being bundled into a van or a truck, very likely with his legs tied together so that he could not kick, and being driven away. If he was at school, he wouldn't have to see any of that or hear Oliver's loud *hrup!*s of anger and distress.

But it was school break.

He dressed and went to let out his birds.

Obedient as always, Oliver followed him from the stable into the orchard and waited expectantly as Jack opened the door of the old shed under the apple tree.

"Ollie! Ollie! Ollie!" shouted the goslings excitedly, and Lydia said, "Good morning, Oliver darling. Would you like to take the children for a walk?"

"Yes, please, Mama," said Oliver eagerly.

"Watch out for foxes, son!" shouted Wilfred. "They'll get a kick out of meeting you!" and he waddled off, cackling loudly at his own wit.

What a happy family they are now, thought Jack. I'm not the only one who's going to miss Oliver dreadfully.

At breakfast the Daw family was not a happy one.

Jack was silent and played with his food, and the others, including Margery, were miserable on his behalf.

"He's taking it hard," said Mrs. Daw afterward, when Jack had gone out to the orchard again.

"It's my fault, really," said Farmer Daw. "I should have made him return Oliver when he was still a chick."

"We could take Jack to visit him at the wildlife park, couldn't we?" asked Margery, but before anyone could answer, they heard a car drive into the yard.

Jack heard it, too, but when he ran to the orchard gate and saw that it was not a truck or a van but a red sports car, he heaved a sigh of relief and went back to Oliver. By now the eight goslings, their walk finished, were swimming on the pond with their parents, and Jack and Oliver stood alone together, the boy's arm around the bird's neck.

Then Farmer Daw came into the orchard, with a small, thin ginger-bearded figure at his side.

"Oh, Oliver," whispered Jack.

He walked forward, the ostrich following, and stopped in front of the director.

"Hello," he said in a flat voice. "This is Oliver."

"Boo!" said Oliver politely. He stretched out his neck and thrust forward his head in a way that to some people might have appeared menacing, but the director merely reached into his pocket, took something out, and offered it to the bird on the flat of his hand.

Delicately, Oliver took it and swallowed it.

"Twoo!" he said.

Jack watched the shape going down Oliver's throat. It looked square.

"What was that?" he said.

103

"A dog biscuit," said the director. "They like them. What have you been feeding him?"

"I started him on chick feed," said Jack, "but he usually shares the wet mash I make up for the geese and ducks. Barley meal and flaked maize mostly—I reckon he gets lots of animal protein when he's foraging, worms and beetles and stuff."

"Good for you," said the director. "You wouldn't have known it, but if you feed ostrich chicks a high-protein diet their bodies get too heavy and they end up with bowlegs. Now, this chap's legs are beautifully straight and strong. In fact, he looks a picture. How does he get on with the rest of the poultry?"

"Oh, fine," said Jack, and he called, "Lydia! Wilfred!"

The white geese came up out of the pond and hastened toward him, shouting their names in reply, while the goslings ran to their big brother, crying, "Ollie! Ollie! Ollie!"

And then Jack and his father told the story of the previous day's drama, and how Oliver had slain the fox.

The director looked thoughtful. "A kick that can kill a fox could do awful damage to a boy, you know, Mr. Daw," he said.

"Oh, Oliver would never hurt Jack!" laughed

Farmer Daw. "He's as obedient as a sheepdog and as quiet as a lamb."

Then a thought struck Jack. If the director was going to take the ostrich away, why was he worrying about Jack getting hurt? If the director was going to take the ostrich away, why hadn't he come with a van or a truck?

"If you're going to take the ostrich away—" he said, but the director interrupted him.

"I'm not," he said.

"You're not!" cried Jack. "You mean. . . ?"

"I mean that, at the moment, I don't want him. We've got a mature male—his father—and several females and a number of youngish chicks at the park right now, and a young male like this wouldn't fit in. The hens would bully him, and as for the cock, he'd give him a really hard time, injure him badly perhaps. At best, he'd be isolated and miserable. Later on, when he's full grown, I may be able to place him at some other safari park, but for the present, there's only one thing that Oliver needs."

Jack licked his lips. "What's that?" he said.

The director looked directly at him, and a small smile appeared on the ginger-bearded face.

"A good home, Jack," he said. "And that, it seems to me, is what he's got."

# 12 Speed Trials

That day, Jack and Oliver were exactly the same height.

After the director had gone, they stood side by side, and Jack's father measured them.

"Dead equal," he said. "Four feet nine. But not for long."

And how right he was.

On Jack's tenth birthday they were measured again, and Jack had grown an inch. Oliver had grown nine.

On the ostrich's second birthday he and Farmer Daw stood side by side, and Jack measured them.

"Dead equal" he said. "Six feet. But not for long."

There was no doubt now that Oliver was a male. Like all his kind, his long neck and his strong legs with their heavily muscled thighs were bare of feathers, but those on his body were now coal black, contrasting strikingly with the snowy white of wing and tail plumes.

Somehow, since the director's visit to the farm, Jack had come to terms with the fact that Oliver was to be his for only a limited time. One day the ostrich would have to go, but in the meantime Jack was determined simply to enjoy his company. And though Oliver was his favorite, he did not neglect his other feathered pets. Jack in fact had become something of a dealer in birds, for such was his success as a breeder, of budgerigars and bantams in particular, that he earned himself some decent pocket money by selling surplus stock.

Lydia and Wilfred's first eight goslings made him a handsome profit when they were old enough to be sold, and by then Lydia had hatched a second brood to run happily about with the giant baby-sitter.

But now Oliver not only looked after them but also began occasionally to treat them to the full courting display of the mature male ostrich. After a series of loud *BOOM!*s, he would sink down, flapping his wings wildly and whipping his head from side to side across the grass. Why he did this, Oliver did not know, nor did the goslings, but they very much enjoyed the show and would applaud it with loud cries of "Ollie! Ollie! Ollie!"

Jack knew, of course: Oliver needed a mate, needed his own flock of hen ostriches. Jack also knew that, when the chance came for the ostrich to have them, he must be happy for Oliver, though he might feel sorry for himself. But still he dreaded a summons from the wildlife park.

Then one evening the phone rang and Jack answered it.

"Is that Jack Daw?" said a voice.

"Yes."

"How's Oliver?"

Jack knew immediately who it was. The voice was not deep enough to be the police sergeant's, and only one other person knew Oliver's name. Jack gulped.

"He's okay." he said. This is it, he thought.

"Good," said the director. "I'm calling you in case you hadn't noticed that there's a wildlife program all about ostriches tonight at 8:30 on Channel 2."

"Oh, thanks!" said Jack.

"Right," said the director. "So long, Jack," and he hung up without another word.

The program was partly about wild ostriches and partly about ostrich farming in South Africa, where the birds were raised in large numbers to be slaughtered for their feathers, for their meat, and for their skins, which were made into a kind of leather. Jack didn't like this part of it at all, but he did like the closing sequence. This was about ostrich racing.

The runners were cocks, each guided by his jockey with reins attached to a kind of halter, and away they all went at tremendous speed.

"Look at that!" said Jack.

"Don't you get any ideas," said his mother.

"You'd fall off, anyway," said his sister.

"Oliver wouldn't let you get on," said his father.

But Oliver did.

The very next day, without telling the others, Jack went out to the orchard, where Oliver was grazing at the far end. At Jack's call, he came cruising up and stood looking down at the boy, fluttering his eyelashes. Lately, Jack had not easily been able to give the ostrich a head-scratching because Oliver was now so tall, and the bird, sensing this, would bend his neck for it. This he now did, but Jack did not comply. Instead he folded his legs beneath him and sat down on the grass. At the same time he patted the ground and said, "Sit!"

Oliver remained standing.

Jack had expected this and now took from his pocket one of the large square dog biscuits that, ever since the director's visit, he had been buying as special treats.

"Sit!" he said again, but although Oliver nuzzled hopefully at the hand that held the biscuit, Jack would not release it.

At last, perhaps by chance, perhaps out of companionship, perhaps because he was tired of standing up, Oliver sat down and was given his reward. Jack made no further move that morning. Like all good animal trainers, he knew that patience was a must, and not until a week later, when he was confident that Oliver would sit on command, did he get to his feet beside the sitting bird and slowly, casually, head-scratching all the time, put one leg across Oliver's back, just for a moment, and then take it away again.

Each day he straddled the sitting ostrich a little longer and then began to put a little weight on his back, gradually, until at last the moment came when he was resting his whole weight on Oliver.

Jack waited, not knowing what to expect.

Would Oliver *hrup!* at him disapprovingly?

Would he jump up and chuck him off?

Or would he just go on sitting there, as he had been told to do?

Oliver did none of these things.

To Jack's delight he rose easily to his feet and began to walk down the orchard like any trained riding ostrich.

From then on it was easy. To ride Oliver was, for Jack, the greatest fun, and he very soon realized that, for Oliver, it was a pleasant task to carry him. Within a week they had progressed from a walk to a gentle trot. Oliver held his head high, his neck curved like a swan's, and Jack sat easily on his back, gripping the bird's body with his knees and balancing himself by holding lightly with his hands on either side of the thick throat. A tap with the heels increased Oliver's speed, and a hand signal—one arm held out sideways—turned him to the left or the right.

There was only one thing wrong, to Jack's mind. They couldn't go fast enough. Oliver was so conditioned to watching where he put his big feet, for fear of stepping on goslings, that he could not be persuaded to run at full speed, which Jack was longing for him to do.

Lydia and Wilfred watched these antics from different points of view. Lydia was no longer astonished at anything that Oliver did. Raising two broods of goslings had convinced her that, whatever he was, he was not of the same species. He was a changeling. Wilfred, however, clung stubbornly to his belief that his son, despite everything, was a gander.

He watched rider and steed with pride. "Remarkable fellow, that son of ours," he said to Lydia. "Carrying the boy on his back! You wouldn't believe any goose could do such a thing, would you?"

"No," said Lydia.

That evening, when the family was swimming on the duck pond, Oliver came up for a drink.

"Come on in, Ollie!" shouted the new goslings. "The water's lovely!"

For the first time in ages Oliver remembered Lydia's words of long ago. "You mustn't go into that pond again until you're much bigger," she had said.

Oliver looked down at his feet. I *am* much bigger, he thought, and he walked gingerly, one slow stride at a time, into the pond. The day had been a hot one, and Oliver waded deeper, enjoying the pleasant sensation of the cool water on his legs, legs now so long that even in the deepest part his body was still above the surface.

He moved around the middle of the pond, and Wilfred cried loudly, "Well done, son, you're swimming at last! You wouldn't believe it, Lydia, would you?"

"No," said Lydia.

The next day Jack got up very early. The time had come, he reckoned, for speed trials, and he did not want anyone to see them.

As the police sergeant had said, the Daws' farm was pretty isolated, and even the nearest country lane was some way away. From it a tarmac farm road led to the house and buildings, and it was along this farm road that Jack planned to give Oliver his test. Sensibly though, he made the first trial on grass.

"That road is hard, you see," he said to Oliver, as he walked him out of the stable, "and I might fall off when you get into top gear."

But in fact he found that the faster Oliver went, the easier it was to ride him, so smooth was that huge, flowing stride. The ostrich seemed to know what was expected of him, and they raced across the biggest of the pastures at a fine rate.

"Now," said Jack, "get your breath, Oliver, be-

cause this is the real trial. The farm road is exactly half a mile long—I made a note of it on the trip in Dad's car the other day—so I can work out your top speed."

Neither *boo!* nor *twoo!* or *hrup!* really served as an answer when Oliver, as now, did not understand what Jack was going on about, but he was fired up by the thrill of a good gallop and he sensed that something challenging was about to happen, so he gave a loud *BOOM!*

Jack rode to the junction where the farm road met the lane, looked cautiously to make sure there was no one about, and then turned the ostrich's head toward the stable. He waited until the second hand on his watch reached 12 and then, with a dig of his heels, he cried, "Go, Oliver! Go!"

And how Oliver went!

His giant strides ate up the ground, and the cows in the neighboring field stampeded wildly as Jack flashed by on his great black-and-white charger.

Somehow he managed to keep his eye on the face of the watch as they sailed through the farm gate (the finishing line), and he saw that the second hand pointed to 9. They had covered the half mile in exactly forty-five seconds.

Ten minutes later, after much chewing on a stub of pencil and many crossed-out sums on the back of an old envelope, Jack came up with the answer: 40 mph!

He had to tell the family, of course. He couldn't possibly keep it to himself any longer, and that afternoon, after school, he repeated the run while they all stood at the gate and goggled in amazement.

His mother spoke for all of them when she said, "I simply don't believe my eyes!"

"I'll do it again," said Jack, and he walked Oliver back to the start.

But on this next run Oliver had just reached full speed when Jack suddenly heard the sound of a car behind him on the farm road and, glancing back, saw it following them.

It was a red sports car, and at the wheel was a small, thin figure with a narrow face and a ginger beard.

# 13 Time Flies

"I simply don't believe my eyes!" said the director to the Daws.

He got out of the red car and walked to meet rider and steed as they came trotting back.

"Hello, Jack," he said.

"Hello," said Jack, nervously.

"And hello, Oliver."

"*Boo-hoo-hoo-hoo,*" said Oliver breathlessly.

"Do you know how fast you were going?" said the director.

"About forty, I expect."

"You expect right. How long have you been riding him?"

"About a week. But I haven't let him go full out before. Today's the first time."

"And the last, I'm afraid," said the director.

He turned to Farmer Daw. "No point in mincing

words, Mr. Daw," he said. "I came to tell you that I need this ostrich. Our cock—his father—is getting on a bit now and so are his hens. I'm sending them all to a safari park that's just starting up, in another part of the country. We're going to begin again, with fresh blood, some new young hens that I've imported. And a new young male."

"Oliver," said Jack.

"I'm afraid so," said the director. "Apart from the fact that I need him, he needs to be with his own kind, you know. Ostriches are flock birds, and it's not natural for him to be on his own."

"I know," said Jack. "He's been displaying a lot lately, and *booming* much more, too. Anyway, he isn't really mine. The egg belonged to you."

He scratched the top of the ostrich's head.

"In some ways Oliver will always be yours," said the director. "I've thought a lot about this, and though I don't see that we need to pay you money for him—strictly speaking, he belongs to Wildlife Park—we certainly need to compensate you. You've done a tremendous job, Jack, to hatch and rear such a magnificent specimen. The least I can do is give you a Life Membership card. That means that you can visit the park, free of charge, whenever you want to."

"You'll still be able to see Oliver as often as you like," said Jack's mother.

"Thank you very much," said Jack. I just wish I'd had longer to ride him, he thought.

"I expect you wish you'd had longer to ride him," said the director.

"Yes."

The director smiled.

"We might be able to arrange that," he said. "Perhaps every now and then your dad could bring you over early, before we open to the public?"

Farmer Daw smiled. "We might be able to arrange that," he said.

The actual parting wasn't as dreadful as Jack had feared. They sent a cattle trailer, so that there would be enough headroom for Oliver to stand comfortably, and Jack persuaded him up the ramp and was waiting at the park to unload him.

Oliver walked sedately down, looked around, and saw, out in the ostrich paddock, a number of strange birds. His great eyes widened as he stared at them in amazement.

Those birds are not like Mama and Papa, he thought.

But *I* am not like Mama and Papa, he thought.

Those birds, he thought, are like me!

With the loudest *boom!* he had ever *boomed,* he ran to meet them.

The director and Farmer Daw and Jack stood watching as Oliver reached his hens. He sank down

before them, flapping his wings wildly and whipping his head from side to side across the grass while each hen ostrich pretended to take no notice but slyly watched the handsome stranger out of the corner of her eye.

"He's happy," said Jack quietly. "Let's go home."

"You'll be able to see him again soon," said his father.

"Time flies," said the director. "You'd be surprised."

Time flew, and Jack was indeed surprised one day when, looking through the diary in which he recorded all the hatchings of all his many different birds, he realized that Lydia and Wilfred's present brood of goslings was their seventh! Five years had flashed by since Oliver had left the farm, five years during which Jack had visited him and his wives and his many children as often as possible, sometimes early, for a ride.

Absence makes the heart grow fonder, they say, and the bond between boy and bird was stronger than ever.

One day he arrived to be told that he was wanted in the director's office.

When he went in, there was a smile on the foxy face. "You're taller every time I see you," said the director. "How much do you reckon you've grown since first we met?"

"About a foot, I think," said Jack.

"Oliver must have grown three feet in that same time," said the director. "Thanks to him—and thanks to you in the first place, of course—we've got a splendid flock of ostriches here now. It's really getting a bit too much for the ranger who looks after them, on top of his other work. He needs someone to help him, someone who could eventually take over the ostriches."

Jack said nothing. His heart was going like a jackhammer.

The director lifted a paw and pulled at that ginger beard, now flecked with gray.

"You'll be leaving school soon?" he said.

"Yes."

"Want a job?"

14 And How!

Beside the ostrich paddock at Wildlife Park a party of schoolchildren was standing, ceaselessly nagging their teacher to allow them to open their packed lunches. ("I'm starving, Miss, it's been more than two hours since I had my breakfast.")

It was the middle of the morning, and beside the information notice was another that said

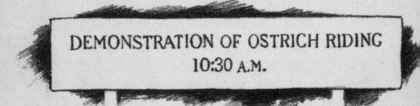

DEMONSTRATION OF OSTRICH RIDING
10:30 A.M.

A lot of people now began to gather, and then, at half past ten, they were joined by one of the park rangers. He seemed very young, not much more than a boy, really, but he called out confidently, "Ladies and gentlemen!" and when he had the crowd's attention, he said, "Good morning, everyone. My name is Jack Daw, and in a moment I'm going to ride our big male ostrich. But before I do, I must warn you all, the younger ones especially, that this is not something that anyone can do. A kick from an ostrich can kill a man. The only reason that I'm able to ride our cock is that I brought him up. I put an ostrich egg under a goose—just as a cuckoo lays her egg in the nest of a hedge sparrow or a wagtail—and that goose hatched out this cuckoo child. And I reared him till he was two years old. Now he's eight, and he weighs 345 pounds, and he stands exactly nine feet tall."

Then the young ranger unlocked a gate in the fence and went in, closing it behind him, and cupped his hands to his mouth and called, "Ol-i-ver!"

In reply there came a noise like the roar of a distant lion, and the people saw a great black-and-white bird half as tall again as a man leave his smaller, grayish wives and come striding across the grass and stop and stand beside the ranger, staring down at him with huge brown eyes.

"*Boo!*" said the giant bird softly.

Then it bent its neck for the ranger to scratch the top of its head.

"*Twoo!*" said Oliver. "*Twoo! Twoo!*" and he fluttered his eyelashes.

"Sit!" said Jack, and Oliver sat and waited till the jockey was mounted.

Then he rose to his full height and began to walk away with long, slow deliberate strides to the far side of the paddock.

Here, bird and rider stopped and turned and stood for a long moment as still as stone, silhouetted against the summer sky.

Then, just as the crowd was beginning to think nothing more would happen, they heard the ranger cry, "Go, Oliver! Go!"

And then how they clapped and cheered!

And how the mighty ostrich ran!

And how still and proud upon his great back sat Jack Daw, who had a way with birds!

And how!

Dick King-Smith has written many highly acclaimed books for young readers. His novel *Babe, the Gallant Pig* received England's 1984 Guardian Award for Excellence in children's literature and was a Boston Globe–Horn Book Honor book. Mr. King-Smith was born and raised in Gloucestershire, England, where he still resides.

Leslie W. Bowman received her B.F.A. from the Rhode Island School of Design. Since 1987, she has illustrated more than ten books for children. This is her first book for Hyperion Books for Children. She lives in Minnesota, with her dog, Jazz.